Dear Parent:

Congratulations! Your child is taking the first steps on an exciting journey. The destination? Independent reading!

STEP INTO READING® will help your child get there. The program offers five steps to reading success. Each step includes fun stories and colorful art. There are also Step into Reading Sticker Books, Step into Reading Math Readers, Step into Reading Phonics Readers, Step into Reading Write-In Readers, and Step into Reading Phonics Boxed Sets—a complete literacy program with something to interest every child.

Learning to Read, Step by Step!

Ready to Read   Preschool–Kindergarten
• big type and easy words • rhyme and rhythm • picture clues
For children who know the alphabet and are eager to begin reading.

Reading with Help   Preschool–Grade 1
• basic vocabulary • short sentences • simple stories
For children who recognize familiar words and sound out new words with help.

Reading on Your Own   Grades 1–3
• engaging characters • easy-to-follow plots • popular topics
For children who are ready to read on their own.

Reading Paragraphs   Grades 2–3
• challenging vocabulary • short paragraphs • exciting stories
For newly independent readers who read simple sentences with confidence.

Ready for Chapters   Grades 2–4
• chapters • longer paragraphs • full-color art
For children who want to take the plunge into chapter books but still like colorful pictures.

STEP INTO READING® is designed to give every child a successful reading experience. The grade levels are only guides. Children can progress through the steps at their own speed, developing confidence in their reading, no matter what their grade.

Remember, a lifetime love of reading starts with a single step!

Step into Reading, Random House, and the Random House colophon are registered trademarks of Random House, Inc.

Visit us on the Web!
StepIntoReading.com
randomhouse.com/kids

Educators and librarians, for a variety of teaching tools, visit us at
randomhouse.com/teachers

ISBN: 978-0-7364-2888-0 (trade) — ISBN: 978-0-7364-8115-1 (lib. bdg.)

Printed in the United States of America   10 9 8 7 6 5 4 3 2

Random House Children's Books supports the First Amendment and celebrates the right to read.

STEP INTO READING®

STEP 2

Disney
PRINCESS

Cinderella

By Melissa Lagonegro
Illustrated by the Disney Storybook Artists

Random House New York

Cinderella is a kind
and pretty girl.
She has many
animal friends.

Cinderella lives
with her mean
stepfamily
and their nasty cat.
She does all the chores.
The stepsisters yell
at Cinderella.

Cinderella's stepmother is Lady Tremaine. She does not like Cinderella.

She gives Cinderella
more chores to do.

The family gets a letter.
The Prince is having
a royal ball!

Everyone in the kingdom
is invited.
Cinderella must finish
her chores
before she can go.

Cinderella finds
an old dress
in the attic.
She can fix it.

She can make it pretty!
Cinderella
and her friends
are excited.

Lady Tremaine gives
Cinderella a pile
of clothes to sew.

Cinderella's friends
fix her dress for her.
The birds add bows.
The mice add ribbons
and beads.

Surprise!
Cinderella loves
her new dress.
Her chores are done.
She can go
to the ball!

Cinderella looks pretty.

Her stepsisters are mad.

They do not want
Cinderella to go
to the ball.
They tear her dress
and pull her beads.

Cinderella is sad.
The Fairy Godmother
appears.

She turns a pumpkin
into a coach.
It will take Cinderella
to the ball!

The Fairy Godmother
gives Cinderella
a sparkling dress
and glass slippers.

Cinderella is ready
for the ball!
She must be home
before the magic stops.

Cinderella arrives
at the palace.
She meets the Prince.
He asks her to dance.

They take a walk.

They fall in love.

It is late!

Cinderella must go.

She runs down the stairs.

She loses a glass slipper.

The magic stops.
Cinderella's dress
and coach change back.
She has one glass slipper.

The Prince's true love
is gone.

He has her glass slipper.

The Prince's father
wants to find her.

Lady Tremaine locks
Cinderella in her room.
She does not want
the Prince to find her.

Cinderella's friends
get the key to her room.
They unlock the door.

Cinderella tries on
the glass slipper.
It fits!
She is the Prince's
true love!

Cinderella
and the Prince
get married.
They live happily
ever after!